Elizabeth of Pemberley

ELIZABETH OF PEMBERLEY

First edition. September 2, 2024.

Copyright © 2024 Darryl Martel.

ISBN: 979-8224557431

Written by Darryl Martel.

Table of Contents

Elizabeth
of
Pemberley

By

Darryl Martel

<u>Prologue</u>

The sweeping hills of Derbyshire gleamed under the soft blush of dawn as Pemberley stood majestic and timeless, its stones weathered yet imperious, like an old soul that had watched centuries pass with quiet dignity. The estate—so grand and vast—now had a new mistress, one whose spirit was as lively as the breeze that danced over the lake and among the trees. Elizabeth Darcy, née Bennet, stood at the threshold of her new life, the great house rising before her, as formidable as the man she had married.

Though she had traversed these halls as a guest, stepping now through the grand oak doors as Mistress of Pemberley was another matter entirely. As Mrs. Reynolds, the venerable housekeeper, welcomed her and her husband with a gracious smile, Elizabeth's heart quickened. Behind her, the line of servants stood in solemn silence, their eyes discreetly assessing the woman who would guide and manage this estate, who would uphold its storied legacy.

The gravity of her new role, as the stewardess of such a place, filled her with both excitement and trepidation. This was no modest household like Longbourn. Pemberley was a world unto itself—rich with history, duty, and expectations. She could almost hear the whispers of those who had come before her: the previous mistresses who had ruled with grace dand authority, whose portraits hung in the long gallery, watching her now.

Yet, beneath the layers of unease, Elizabeth's eyes sparkled with determination. She was no stranger to challenges, nor to navigating unfamiliar worlds. Though her upbringing was humbler than that of her new station, she knew herself to be capable—her wit and character having already won over the most difficult of men: Mr. Fitzwilliam Darcy, the very embodiment of Pemberley's grandeur.

Darcy's presence beside her, tall and resolute, provided an unexpected comfort. His love had softened the walls of this house in her mind, turning Pemberley from a cold, daunting fortress into a place where her heart could belong. His touch at her elbow, reassuring and familiar, reminded her that she was not alone in this new chapter of her life. Together, they would navigate the intricacies of their roles—not as Master and Mistress alone, but as partners, their bond as steady as the stone that built the home they now shared.

The challenge ahead was great, and Elizabeth knew that the path of a mistress was not always lined with the joy and ease she might wish for. There would be expectations to meet, judgments to navigate, and a household of souls who would look to her for guidance and care. But there would also be moments of triumph, of discovery, and of the quiet contentment she had already begun to glimpse.

As she stepped through the doors of Pemberley, her heart a thrilling blend of fear and excitement, Elizabeth Darcy knew that this new life—this new identity as Mistress of Pemberley—would demand all of her courage, her wit, and her spirit.

And she was ready.

Chapter 1
Elizabeth of Pemberley

A New Beginning

As the carriage rumbled up the winding path that led to Pemberley's grand entrance, Elizabeth Darcy sat beside her husband, her hand resting in his, her heart beating in rhythm with the horses' hooves. The sight of Pemberley, as it rose from the lush green landscape, filled her with awe once more. She had seen it before, admired it from afar, but today it felt different. Today, it was to become her home.

Fitzwilliam Darcy glanced at her, a flicker of emotion crossing his usually composed face. His eyes softened, as if he understood the storm of thoughts racing through her mind. "You will be perfect," he said quietly, squeezing her hand in reassurance.

Elizabeth gave him a grateful smile, though her nerves fluttered in her chest. She could see, as they neared the entrance, the entire household staff standing at attention, a line of uniformed figures that stretched up the stone steps, all waiting. At the top, under the imposing arch of the door, stood three familiar faces. Mrs. Reynolds, the ever-dignified housekeeper, was there, her expression warm and welcoming. Beside her was the butler, solemn and precise as always. But Elizabeth's eyes were drawn to the figure standing between them—Georgiana Darcy, her husband's beloved younger sister, who now wore a smile as bright as the sun.

The carriage came to a stop, and the driver leapt down to open the door. Darcy was the first to step out, his tall frame casting a long shadow across the cobblestones. He turned and offered his hand to Elizabeth, helping her down with the same care and attention he had shown since the day they had married. She took a deep breath, her feet now on the ground of what would be her new life.

As they approached the waiting crowd of servants, Elizabeth felt their eyes on her. Some were curious, others respectful, and a few perhaps carried the weight of judgment, assessing whether this lively, strong-willed woman from Hertfordshire could truly fit into the grand world of Pemberley. She straightened her shoulders, determined not to let the magnitude of this moment unsettle her.

Mrs. Reynolds stepped forward, her kindly face alight with genuine warmth. She curtsied deeply to Darcy and then to Elizabeth, her voice steady as she spoke.

"Welcome home, Mr. Darcy. And welcome, Mrs. Darcy, to Pemberley. We are honoured to have you as our Mistress."

Elizabeth returned the smile, her tension easing slightly at the housekeeper's kindness. "Thank you, Mrs. Reynolds. I am delighted to be here."

Georgiana could not wait any longer. Breaking from her place beside the butler, she rushed forward, her joy unmistakable. "Elizabeth! Oh, I am so happy you are here." She threw her arms around Elizabeth, who laughed softly at the younger girl's exuberance. Georgiana's embrace was genuine, filled with affection that Elizabeth had come to cherish during their growing friendship.

"My dear Georgiana," Elizabeth said, her voice warm, "I am so happy to see you."

Darcy, watching the exchange with a small, affectionate smile, stepped forward and placed a hand on his sister's shoulder. "You must give Elizabeth some air, Georgiana," he teased gently. "She has only just arrived."

Georgiana laughed softly, stepping back but keeping her hands on Elizabeth's. "I have been waiting all morning for your arrival. Pemberley has missed you, Brother, and I... I have missed you both."

Elizabeth's heart swelled at the welcome. Though the grandeur of Pemberley still loomed around her, daunting in its size and history, the warmth of those she cared about softened its intimidating presence. She felt, in that moment, a part of something larger, something she could help build and nurture.

As they stood together, Darcy turned to address the assembled staff, his voice deep and clear. "You all know my sister, and I trust you will come to know and respect my wife as you have done with me. Mrs. Darcy is now the mistress of Pemberley. I expect you will give her the same loyalty and care that you have shown to me."

There was a murmur of respectful agreement from the staff, though Elizabeth could feel the weight of their expectations settle on her shoulders. It was not just Pemberley she had to learn, but the lives of those who worked within it—the people who would now look to her for guidance and leadership.

With the formalities complete, Mrs. Reynolds stepped forward again, her voice as steady as ever. "Shall I show you to your rooms, Mr. Darcy, Mrs. Darcy? Everything has been prepared for your arrival."

Darcy glanced at Elizabeth, his expression asking the silent question of whether she was ready to step fully into her new role. She nodded, her confidence returning. "Yes, Mrs. Reynolds. I think I would like that very much."

They made their way up the wide stone steps, the staff bowing or curtseyed as they ascended. Elizabeth, felt the eyes of the house upon her, watching her every step. But with Darcy beside her and Georgiana beaming at her side, she found her nerves easing. She had made it through the first steps of her new life as Mistress of Pemberley, and she knew that though there would be challenges ahead, she would meet them with courage and grace.

The doors of Pemberley opened wide, and Elizabeth Darcy, with her husband's hand in hers, crossed the threshold into her new life.

As the new Mistress of Pemberley, Elizabeth was acutely aware of the expectations that rested upon her shoulders. The estate was not just a home, it was an institution, a legacy that had been meticulously preserved by the Darcy family for generations. Her role was not merely that of a wife but as a steward of this legacy.

From the moment of her engagement to Mr. Fitzwilliam Darcy, the responsibilities that awaited her had been a frequent topic of conversation. Society held high expectations for the Mistress of Pemberley. She was to be a paragon of grace, hospitality, and competence. Elizabeth knew that every decision she made, every word she spoke, and every action she took would be scrutinised by both the servants within the household and the society outside.

The estate itself demanded meticulous management. The staff, the grounds, the tenants, and the social engagements all required her attention. Elizabeth had observed her mother's management of Longbourn, but she understood that Pemberley operated on an entirely different scale. The expectations of the Darcy name were immense, and she was determined not to falter under their weight.

Despite her determination, Elizabeth could not shake her worries and concerns. She feared that her lack of experience might lead to mistakes that could tarnish the reputation of Pemberley. The fear of failing her husband, who had shown unwavering faith in her abilities, was a constant shadow.

Elizabeth was also keenly aware that some might question her suitability for the role. Her relatively modest background and the less refined manners of her family were points of potential criticism.

In quieter moments, Elizabeth wondered if she could truly belong in a world so vastly different from her own upbringing. The opulence of Pemberley, with its priceless artworks and sprawling gardens, seemed almost surreal.

She worried about managing the household staff, most of whom had been at Pemberley for years, if not decades. Would they respect her authority? Would they accept her as their new mistress?

As Elizabeth stepped inside the grand hall of Pemberley, she couldn't help but pause, taking in the immense beauty that surrounded her. The sun streamed through tall, arched windows, casting warm light across the polished floors and gleaming wood paneling. A magnificent chandelier hung from the ceiling, its crystals twinkling like stars. The elegance of the house felt overwhelming for a moment, but Elizabeth knew she must not let it overtake her. Pemberley was not just a symbol of wealth and grandeur, it was to be her home.

Mrs. Reynolds led them through the hall, the staff having dispersed to attend to their duties now that the initial welcome was complete. Darcy walked beside her, his presence both calming and reassuring, while Georgiana trailed behind, occasionally pointing out small details about the house with childlike enthusiasm. Elizabeth listened with a fond smile, though her attention remained primarily on Mrs. Reynolds, who was explaining the household arrangements.

"Mrs. Darcy," Mrs. Reynolds began, turning to her with the grace and dignity of a woman who had long managed this household, "allow me to introduce you to your lady's maid, Mrs. Jennings."

From the shadow of a nearby doorway stepped a woman in her late twenties, modestly dressed but with an air of quiet competence about her. Her brown hair was neatly tucked beneath a simple cap, and her eyes, though downcast at first, met Elizabeth's with a look of respect and interest. She curtsied, her hands folded demurely in front of her.

"Mrs. Darcy," Mrs. Jennings said softly, her voice smooth and even. "It is a pleasure to be at your service."

Elizabeth regarded her for a moment, unsure how she felt about having someone attend to her so personally. She had never been the sort to need constant assistance, nor had she grown up in a household where a personal maid was anything but a luxury beyond reach. Yet, she knew this was expected of her now, and she hoped to manage this new relationship with warmth and understanding, rather than distant formality.

"Thank you, Mrs. Jennings," Elizabeth said kindly, her smile reaching her eyes. "I look forward to working with you. I hope we shall come to understand one another well."

Mrs. Jennings gave a slight nod, and there was a glimmer of something in her expression—perhaps relief, or even hope. "I will endeavour to do my best to serve you, Mrs. Darcy. I have heard much about your spirit and grace."

Elizabeth raised an eyebrow in surprise. "I hope what you have heard has not raised your expectations too high," she said with a laugh. "I am far from perfect, as you will soon discover."

The maid smiled, her manner softening just a little. "I expect that is what will make working with you all the more pleasant, ma'am."

Elizabeth was touched by the response and felt her initial reservations fading. She could see in Mrs. Jennings someone she might trust, and perhaps, over time, even form a friendship with, despite the difference in their stations. There was no air of haughty superiority in the maid's manner, only a quiet competence and a hint of sincerity that Elizabeth appreciated.

Turning slightly to Mrs. Reynolds, Elizabeth said, "Thank you for the introduction. I am certain Mrs. Jennings and I will come to work well together."

Mrs. Reynolds, ever the picture of efficiency and grace, smiled gently. "I have no doubt, Mrs. Darcy. Mrs. Jennings has served in Pemberley for many years and is well-regarded. If you require anything, she will always be at your beck and call, as is the custom."

Elizabeth gave a small nod, but inside, she hoped she could build more of a partnership with Mrs. Jennings than the rigid hierarchy suggested. She was not one to relish the idea of someone constantly attending her every need, and though it was new for her, she wanted the people of Pemberley to feel valued, respected, and comfortable in their roles. The idea of forming a bond—one of trust and mutual understanding—appealed to her more than a cold, distant relationship where titles defined the limits of connection.

As they continued deeper into the house, Darcy excused himself to attend to some business matters that required his immediate attention. Elizabeth glanced after him, feeling a pang of nervousness as he disappeared down a long corridor. But Georgiana remained beside her, bright and chatty, clearly excited to show Elizabeth more of the house she now called home.

They reached Elizabeth's private chambers, which Mrs. Reynolds had arranged with meticulous care. The room was spacious and tastefully decorated, with large windows overlooking the rolling hills of the Pemberley estate. Soft fabrics draped the bed and furniture, and a writing desk stood by the window, its surface neatly prepared for use. It was more luxurious than anything Elizabeth had ever known, but somehow, it already felt welcoming.

Mrs. Jennings followed them in, standing by the door as Mrs. Reynolds began to show Elizabeth where everything was stored.

Elizabeth took it all in, silently marvelling at the extent of the preparation that had gone into making her feel welcome.

Once Mrs. Reynolds finished her tour of the chambers, she smiled and curtsied again. "I shall leave you to settle in, Mrs. Darcy. Mrs. Jennings will be here if you require anything, and I shall be just downstairs should you need me." With that, she left the room, her footsteps fading softly down the corridor.

Elizabeth turned to Mrs. Jennings, who remained by the door, her hands clasped lightly in front of her. "Thank you for waiting, Mrs. Jennings. I imagine this will be quite an adjustment for both of us," she said with a gentle laugh, hoping to lighten the mood. "I shall try not to trouble you too much."

The maid gave a small smile in return. "It will be no trouble at all, Mrs. Darcy. My role is to make things easier for you, and I do hope we can work together comfortably."

Elizabeth nodded, her warmth returning in full force. "I hope so, too. And, if I may say, I would prefer that we speak openly. I would rather us be friendly than overly formal. If we are to work together, I should like us to get to know each other a little better."

Mrs. Jennings blinked, clearly taken aback by Elizabeth's openness. "You are very kind, ma'am. I appreciate your consideration."

Elizabeth smiled, feeling a growing sense of ease. "We'll make a fine team, Mrs. Jennings. I have much to learn, but with your help, I am sure we will manage splendidly."

The two women exchanged a glance of mutual understanding, and Elizabeth felt a spark of optimism. Though her role at Pemberley was daunting, she would not face it alone. With Darcy at her side,

Georgiana as a friend, and the steady support of Mrs. Reynolds and Mrs. Jennings, Elizabeth felt more ready than ever to embrace her new life.

Elizabeth found an invaluable ally in Mrs. Reynolds, the housekeeper. Mrs. Reynolds, who had served the Darcy family for many years, she was a woman of formidable capability and deep loyalty. From their first meeting, Elizabeth sensed a kindred spirit in the housekeeper's calm and manner. Mrs. Reynolds' familiarity with every aspect of the estate and her deep respect for Mr. Darcy were immediately evident.

Mrs. Reynolds provided Elizabeth with a comprehensive understanding of the workings of Pemberley. She guided her through the management of the household staff, introduced her to the various responsibilities of maintaining the estate, and offered insights into the personalities and needs of the tenants. Her assistance was not only practical but also comforting. Elizabeth found solace in Mrs. Reynolds' steady presence and her willingness to share her wisdom.

"Mrs. Darcy, if I may offer a word of advice," Mrs. Reynolds had said one afternoon, "it is to trust your instincts. You have a good heart and a keen mind. The rest will follow."

These words of encouragement were a balm to Elizabeth's anxious heart. With Mrs. Reynolds by her side, she felt more confident in her ability to navigate her new role.

The servants at Pemberley, from the footmen to the maids, were initially curious and somewhat skeptical about their new mistress. They had heard rumours of Elizabeth's spirited nature and her lack of a substantial dowry. Some wondered how she would adjust to the grandeur and responsibilities of Pemberley, coming from a much smaller estate.

However, as Elizabeth began to interact with them, their reservations gradually dissipated. She treated each member of the staff with genuine kindness and respect. Elizabeth made it a point to learn their names, inquire about their families, and show appreciation for their hard work. Her efforts did not go unnoticed. The staff began to speak favourably of her, remarking on her warmth and approachability.

"She's different from what I expected," one of the footmen confided to a colleague. "There's a sincerity in her that you don't often see in ladies of her station."

The maids, too, found her manner refreshing. Unlike some mistresses who were distant and imperious, Elizabeth's friendliness made them feel valued.

They were particularly impressed by her willingness to involve herself in the day-to-day running of the household, rather than simply delegating tasks from a distance.

"She's not above lending a hand or listening to a suggestion," one of the maids remarked. "It's clear she cares about Pemberley and everyone in it."

<u>Lady Catherine de Bourgh</u>

However, not everyone was pleased with Elizabeth's new position. Lady Catherine de Bourgh, Mr. Darcy's formidable aunt, made no effort to conceal her disapproval. From the moment she had learned of the engagement, Lady Catherine had been vocal in her objections. She had envisioned a different match for her nephew, someone of higher birth and greater wealth.

During a visit to Pemberley, Lady Catherine did not hesitate to express her disdain. Her words were sharp, her manner condescending. She questioned Elizabeth's ability to manage such a grand estate and insinuated that she was unworthy of the Darcy name.

"I must say, Mrs. Darcy," Lady Catherine said with a thinly veiled sneer, "I had hoped for someone with more… refinement to take on the responsibilities of Pemberley."

Elizabeth, though hurt by the remarks, maintained her composure. She understood that earning Lady Catherine's approval might be an insurmountable task. Nevertheless, she resolved to prove through her actions that she was indeed worthy of her new title and the responsibilities it entailed.

Beyond the walls of Pemberley, society watched Elizabeth with a mixture of curiosity and judgment. The marriage of Mr. Darcy, one of Derbyshire's most eligible bachelors, to Elizabeth Bennet, a lady of comparatively modest means, was a subject of much gossip. Some admired the match, seeing it as a testament to true love conquering societal expectations. Others, however, were less charitable, viewing it as a misstep for a man of Darcy's standing.

Elizabeth faced these judgments with a mixture of resilience and vulnerability. She was aware that her every move was being scrutinised, that her behaviour would be compared unfavourably to the idealised image of what a Mistress of Pemberley should be. She leaned on the support of her husband, whose unwavering confidence in her bolstered her spirits.

"Let them talk," Darcy would often say. "What matters is our happiness and the respect we have for each other."

Despite the societal pressures, Elizabeth found moments of genuine joy in her new life. The beauty of Pemberley, the love she shared with her husband, and the satisfaction of gradually mastering her new responsibilities brought her a deep sense of fulfilment.

As the day of the grand ball approached, Elizabeth found herself both excited and apprehensive. This would be her formal introduction to the world as the Mistress of Pemberley, a title that still felt strange on her lips. The upcoming event had stirred the estate into a whirlwind of preparations—flowers were arranged in every corner, musicians rehearsed in the ballroom, and servants scurried to ensure every detail was perfect.

Elizabeth, who had grown up in a modest country home, had never imagined herself at the centre of such an event. Balls had always been a part of her life, but never as the hostess of one so grand. The weight of expectation pressed down on her. This was not just any gathering; it was the introduction of the new Mistress of Pemberley to the world, and all the most important families of Derbyshire, along with guests from London and beyond, had been invited. Each of them would scrutinise her, would weigh her against the grandeur of the estate and the name Darcy. Would she be enough?

In the days leading up to the ball, Elizabeth sought guidance from those who knew Pemberley best. Darcy, ever her greatest source of strength, was patient and reassuring, helping her navigate the complexities of planning such an event. He had little interest in the trivialities of flowers or the seating arrangements, but he knew well the importance of decorum, and he understood the intricacies of their social world.

"You need not worry, Elizabeth," he said one evening as they walked the grounds together. "You have nothing to prove to anyone. Pemberley stands tall because of who we are—not because of the opinions of those who walk through its doors for one evening."

Elizabeth smiled at him, grateful for his steady support. "That may be true, but I cannot help but feel the weight of it all. This is more than just a ball, is it not? It is our first event as husband and wife. I want it to reflect us—our values, our love for this place."

Darcy stopped and turned to face her, taking her hands in his. "And it will. Because you are its Mistress now, and everything you touch bears your warmth, your intelligence, and your kindness. That is what people will see."

His words soothed her nerves, though a small flutter of anxiety still remained. "Thank you, Fitzwilliam. You always know how to calm me."

Later, Elizabeth sought the practical wisdom of Mrs. Reynolds, whose experience in managing Pemberley was invaluable. Together, they walked through the ballroom, discussing the arrangements. Elizabeth, always mindful of how the servants might feel, took Mrs. Reynolds' advice to heart, trusting her instincts and long years of service.

"You've hosted many a ball here, Mrs. Reynolds," Elizabeth said as they stood by the large windows overlooking the gardens. "What would you suggest? I wish for it to be grand, yes, but also welcoming."

Mrs. Reynolds smiled warmly, clearly pleased by Elizabeth's respect for her counsel. "You are right to want that balance, ma'am. Pemberley is a grand estate, but it is also a home. The best balls are those where guests feel both awe and comfort. I would suggest a touch of elegance in every detail, but nothing too ostentatious. The guests will come expecting splendour, but it is the warmth of the hospitality that will linger in their minds."

Elizabeth nodded thoughtfully. "And you will guide the staff, as you always do?"

"Of course, Mrs. Darcy. They respect you already, you know. And by the end of the evening, so will all your guests."

The night of the ball arrived sooner than Elizabeth expected. The house was transformed—its halls glittering with candlelight, flowers filling the air with a soft, fragrant scent. The ballroom was resplendent, its polished floors gleaming beneath the grand chandelier, while the soft strains of a string quartet played in the background.

Elizabeth stood in her chambers, her hands trembling slightly as Mrs. Jennings adjusted the delicate folds of her gown. The dress was a rich ivory silk, simple yet elegant, a reflection of Elizabeth's taste. It was adorned with fine lace at the neckline and sleeves, and her dark curls had been swept up into an intricate style, a few loose strands falling softly around her face.

Mrs. Jennings stepped back, admiring her work. "You look beautiful, Mrs. Darcy."

Elizabeth smiled, but the knot in her stomach remained. "Thank you, Mrs. Jennings. I only hope I can live up to the expectations."

As if sensing her unease, Mrs. Jennings said quietly, "Pemberley has never looked more beautiful than it does tonight, ma'am, but none of it will shine as brightly as you and Mr. Darcy."

Just then, there was a gentle knock at the door, and Darcy entered. For a moment, he simply stood in the doorway, his eyes lingering on Elizabeth, his expression unreadable.

"You take my breath away," he said softly, crossing the room to her side.

Elizabeth blushed, feeling the heat rise to her cheeks. "You are far too kind," she murmured, but her heart lifted at his words.

He took her hand and placed a gentle kiss on her knuckles. "You have nothing to fear tonight. I will be by your side through every moment."

They descended the grand staircase together, the hum of conversation growing louder as they neared the ballroom. Elizabeth's heart raced, but with Darcy's strong presence beside her, she felt a surge of courage. As they entered the room, all eyes turned toward them. The music softened, and the guests bowed and curtsied in respect.

Elizabeth's breath caught for a moment. This was it—the world's gaze was upon her. But then, she felt Darcy's hand tighten slightly around hers, grounding her. His strength, his confidence, flowed into her.

They moved through the room, greeting their guests. Elizabeth smiled, exchanged pleasantries, and allowed herself to be drawn into conversation, though her mind was still whirring with nerves. Yet, with each passing moment, she began to relax. The atmosphere was lively, and soon, laughter and music filled the air.

As they made their way to the centre of the room for the first dance, Elizabeth looked up at Darcy. His eyes were filled with pride and affection, and in that moment, the grandeur of Pemberley and the weight of the evening faded away. It was just the two of them—partners, equals, and now husband and wife, facing the world together.

The music began, and they moved as one, gliding across the floor. Elizabeth could feel the eyes of the room upon them, but for the first time that evening, she did not care. With Darcy's arm around her, she felt invincible.

When the dance ended, the applause was warm and genuine. Elizabeth curtsied, her heart full, and as she stood tall beside her husband, she realised that this was not just a ball, not just an introduction to society. It was the beginning of her new life at Pemberley—a life she would share with the man she loved, and a home she would care for with all her heart.

For the rest of the evening, as Elizabeth mingled with the guests, laughter on her lips and confidence in her step, she knew that Pemberley had truly become her own.

<u>Confessions to Jane</u>

Two months into her new role, Elizabeth received a most welcome visitor, her beloved sister Jane. The sisters had always shared a close bond, and Elizabeth had missed Jane's calming presence and wise counsel. Jane's visit was a breath of fresh air, a reminder of home and simpler times.

As they walked through the verdant gardens of Pemberley, Elizabeth poured out her heart to Jane. She spoke of her worries and fears, her triumphs and struggles. Jane listened with her usual patience and understanding, offering words of encouragement and support. Herself being the same position, so knew how Elizabeth was feeling.

"I knew you would thrive here, Lizzy," Jane said with a reassuring smile. "You have always been strong and capable. Pemberley is fortunate to have you."

Elizabeth told Jane about her holding the welfare of the servants in high regard, approached Mrs. Reynolds with a request to inspect the servants' quarters. Though an unusual request, Elizabeth's genuine concern for the well-being of the household staff shone through. She aimed to ensure they were well looked after and intended to make any necessary suggestions for improvements. Mr. Darcy, supportive of his wife's compassionate nature,

readily agreed to her proposal, and Mrs. Reynolds, though initially surprised, obliged. The servants, taken aback by the unprecedented visit, found the new mistress's attentiveness both strange and heartening, as they could not recall such an interest in their living conditions from previous mistresses of Pemberley.

"They are very fortunate Lizzy! Most people do not always know who their staff are, being such things are left to the Butler and the Housekeeper." Jane slipped her arm through Lizzie's as they continued their walk.

Elizabeth felt a sense of relief in confiding in Jane. She had missed the ease of their conversations, the comfort of sharing her thoughts and feelings without reservation.

As they strolled through the estate, Jane shared her own experiences as the new Mistress of Netherfield Park Park. Like Elizabeth, she had faced her share of challenges and adjustments. Managing a large household, overseeing social engagements, and navigating the expectations of her new social circle had been daunting tasks.

"But Charles has been wonderful," Jane said, her eyes shining with happiness. "He has been supportive and understanding, much like your Mr. Darcy."

The sisters laughed and commiserated over the peculiarities of their new roles. They exchanged stories of minor mishaps and moments of doubt, finding solace in the knowledge that they were not alone in their experiences.

As their conversation turned more intimate, Jane hesitated for a moment before sharing a piece of news that she had been holding close to her heart.

"Lizzy," Jane began, her voice tinged with excitement and a hint of nervousness, "I have something to tell you. I am with child."

Elizabeth's face lit up with joy. "Oh, Jane! That is wonderful news! I am so happy for you."

Jane's eyes filled with tears of happiness. "I am due in September. Charles and I are overjoyed, but I must admit, I am also a little apprehensive. There is so much to prepare for, and I worry about being a good mother."

Elizabeth took Jane's hands in hers. "You will be a wonderful mother, Jane. Your kindness, patience, and love will guide you. And you have Charles by your side. Together, you will create a beautiful family."

The sisters embraced, their bond stronger than ever. Elizabeth felt a renewed sense of hope and determination. The future, with all its uncertainties, seemed a little less daunting with Jane by her side.

The Bennett's Come to Pemberley

A few days after Jane's departure from Pemberley, Elizabeth found herself seated in the light-filled morning room, her favourite spot for writing. The large windows offered a sweeping view of the gardens, where the late Winter grasses danced gently in the breeze. The serenity of Pemberley was beginning to feel familiar to her, like a soft embrace that reminded her of how far she had come from the noisy chaos of Longbourn. With a sense of contentment, she dipped her quill into ink and began to write a letter to her parents.

"My dearest Mama and Papa," she began, the words flowing easily. _"I hope this letter finds you in good health and spirits. I have been thinking of you often, especially after the wonderful news of Jane's happiness. How fortunate she is to have found such a loving, kind man in Mr. Bingley, and I could not be more pleased for her."_

She paused, smiling as she thought of her sister's recent visit. Jane had been radiant, full of joy and affection for her new life with Mr. Bingley, and their time together had reminded Elizabeth of the strength of their bond. Though they were now both married and living in different households, their closeness remained unchanged.

Elizabeth continued writing, eager to share more of her life at Pemberley with her parents.

"I find myself settling in more with each passing day. Pemberley is grand, of course, but also welcoming, and I have begun to feel its rhythms. The staff have been kind and helpful, especially Mrs. Reynolds, who has shown me great patience as I learn the many responsibilities of my new role. Darcy, too, has been my greatest comfort and guide, always by my side with encouragement and care. I cannot imagine being anywhere else now."

The truth of those words filled her heart with warmth. Pemberley was becoming home in ways she hadn't anticipated. Though its size and grandeur had initially overwhelmed her, Elizabeth was beginning to feel a sense of belonging. She found peace in its gardens, joy in its library, and quiet strength in its halls. And of course, Darcy's unwavering presence made the transition all the easier.

"I would dearly love for you both, along with my sisters, to visit Pemberley soon," she wrote. _"There is so much I wish to show you—the beautiful gardens, the grand rooms, and the tranquil countryside. It would mean the world to me to have you here, so you might see this place that is now my home."_

As she penned the invitation, Elizabeth wondered how her parents might respond. Her father, with his wry sense of humour, would no doubt take pleasure in seeing the grand estate that now belonged to his second daughter. Her mother, however, would be beside herself with excitement, eager to parade around Pemberley and bask in the accomplishment of having married off two daughters so advantageously. Elizabeth smiled to herself at the thought, knowing that, despite her mother's excitable nature, she would welcome the visit with open arms.

"I know you will be delighted with Pemberley, Mama," Elizabeth continued. _"It is a place of elegance and beauty, but also a home where love and respect flourish. I am eager for you to meet the people here, especially Mrs. Reynolds, who I believe you will find most agreeable."_

She thought for a moment about Lydia and Kitty, her younger sisters, and how they would likely react to Pemberley's splendour. Kitty, though often quiet in the shadow of Lydia, might enjoy the peace of the estate, while Lydia—well, Elizabeth could already picture Lydia's excitement at the prospect of exploring the grand rooms and possibly causing some harmless mischief.

"I trust Kitty and Lydia are well," she wrote with affection. _"Tell them I expect them to be on their best behaviour when they visit, as Pemberley has quite a different atmosphere from Longbourn. I will leave it to your discretion, Mama, whether they are ready for such a change of scenery."_

She imagined her father's laugh at that line, and it lightened her heart. Though she had come to love Pemberley, a part of her still missed the liveliness and simplicity of her family at Longbourn—the teasing conversations, the noise of daily life, and even her mother's endless talk of marriages and prospects. Yet, here she was, married to the man she loved, standing at the helm of one of the grandest estates in Derbyshire. Life had taken a path she had never imagined, but it was one she embraced wholeheartedly.

"I will write again soon and hope to hear from you all before long. Please send my love to Jane and Mr. Bingley, and to Mary, Kitty, and Lydia. I eagerly await your visit and hope it will be soon. There is much for us to share and celebrate."

With a final flourish of her quill, Elizabeth signed the letter, feeling a surge of contentment. She folded the paper neatly and sealed it with wax, pressing Darcy's family crest into the warm red wax with a practiced hand. For a moment, she held the letter, her thoughts drifting to her family and the life she had led before this new chapter began. Though Longbourn would always hold a special place in her heart, Pemberley had become her future—one filled with love, purpose, and endless possibilities.

As Elizabeth set the letter aside, she glanced out the window once more, her eyes resting on the gardens where Darcy was walking with Georgiana. The sight filled her with a sense of peace, and she rose from her chair, preparing to join them. Pemberley, with its endless beauty and responsibilities, had become her world. But no matter how grand the estate, it was the people within it—her husband, her family, and her friends—that made it truly home.

With a light step, Elizabeth left the morning room, her thoughts already turning to the future and the visit that would soon bring her family to Pemberley.

The Invitation

Mrs. Bennet could barely contain her excitement when Elizabeth's letter arrived at Longbourn. She had been eagerly awaiting news from her daughter, now Mistress of Pemberley, and the invitation to visit such a grand estate filled her with a mixture of pride and exhilaration. She rushed to Mr. Bennet's study, waving the letter in her hand, her voice high-pitched with delight.

"Mr. Bennet! Oh, Mr. Bennet, you will never believe it! Our dear Lizzy has invited us to visit Pemberley!" she exclaimed, bursting into his room without knocking, as was her usual custom.

Mr. Bennet looked up from his book, his eyebrows raised in mild amusement. "Has she now? Well, that is indeed something," he said with a chuckle. "I suppose you are already planning your attire and packing your trunks as we speak?"

Mrs. Bennet ignored the dry humour in his tone, too absorbed in her own thoughts. "Oh, Mr. Bennet, can you imagine it? Pemberley! The grandest estate in Derbyshire, and our Lizzy is its mistress! We shall stay in rooms finer than we've ever seen, dine in luxury, and walk through the most magnificent gardens!" She fluttered around the room in excitement, the letter clutched in her hand. "And to think, two daughters so well married! What a triumph!"

Mr. Bennet leaned back in his chair, smiling at his wife's exuberance. "Yes, quite a triumph indeed. But I must warn you, my dear, we are going to visit our daughter, not a spectacle. I trust you will remember that while we are at Pemberley?"

Mrs. Bennet waved her hand dismissively. "Of course, of course! I shall behave perfectly! But oh, what joy it will be to see dear Lizzy in such a grand home. I cannot wait!"

She replied to Elizabeth's letter at once, accepting the invitation with all the enthusiasm she could muster. Within days, the Bennet household was in a flurry of preparation for their journey to Pemberley. Mrs. Bennet fussed over what to wear, making sure her finest dresses were packed, while Lydia and Kitty begged to join, only to be reminded by their mother that this visit was strictly for their father and herself. They would have their chance later, Mrs. Bennet assured them, when they were married well enough to merit such invitations.

When the day of their arrival at Pemberley came, Elizabeth stood on the grand steps of the house, Darcy by her side. She watched the carriage approach with a mixture of excitement and trepidation. As much as she loved her family, she knew that Pemberley was a world apart from Longbourn, and she could only hope that her mother's excitable nature and her father's sharp wit would not create any embarrassing scenes. Still, she was eager to see them, and her heart warmed at the thought of sharing her new home with the people she loved.

As the carriage pulled up, Mrs. Bennet was the first to emerge, her eyes wide with awe as she took in the grandeur of Pemberley. "Oh, Lizzy!" she cried as she hurried forward, her voice ringing out with excitement. "My dear, dear Lizzy! Look at this place! How splendid it is! What a life you must lead here!"

Elizabeth smiled warmly, though she felt a flicker of apprehension at her mother's loud exclamations. "Mama, it is so good to see you," she said, embracing her mother. "I'm so pleased you could come."

Mr. Bennet followed at a more leisurely pace, his eyes scanning the estate with an appreciative nod. "Well, Lizzy, it appears you've done quite well for yourself," he remarked, his tone dry but affectionate. "Pemberley is truly a remarkable place."

"Thank you, Papa," Elizabeth said, smiling at her father's understated approval. "I hope you and Mama will enjoy your stay."

Darcy stepped forward then, greeting Mr. Bennet with a polite bow and offering his hand. "Mr. Bennet, Mrs. Bennet, welcome to Pemberley. We are delighted to have you as our guests."

Mrs. Bennet curtsied deeply, her cheeks flushed with excitement. "Oh, Mr. Darcy, we are most honoured to be here! What a magnificent home you have! I can scarcely believe our Lizzy is mistress of all this!"

Darcy smiled politely, though Elizabeth could sense his amusement at Mrs. Bennet's exuberance. "You are most welcome, Mrs. Bennet," he said graciously. "Pemberley is indeed an estate I am proud of, but it is Elizabeth who brings it true life."

Elizabeth glanced at him, her heart swelling with affection for his kind words. He had grown accustomed to her family's quirks, and she appreciated the effort he made to put her mother at ease.

As they made their way into the house, Mrs. Bennet's eyes darted around, taking in every detail. The grand staircase, the chandeliers, the polished floors—all of it seemed to enchant her. "Such elegance!" she whispered in awe. "Oh, Lizzy, you must be the envy of all Derbyshire!"

Elizabeth could not help but laugh softly. "I think I am fortunate, Mama, but it is not the house that brings me happiness. It is the people within it."

Mrs. Bennet beamed at her daughter, though her attention quickly shifted to Darcy, as she launched into a stream of praises.

Elizabeth led them through the house, showing them the rooms that had become her sanctuary—her writing desk in the morning room, the elegant drawing room where she and Georgiana often played music, and the gardens where she and Darcy walked in the evenings. Her mother's delight was palpable, though Elizabeth noticed Mr. Bennet's subtle amusement at his wife's endless commentary.

As they settled in for tea later that afternoon, Elizabeth found herself relaxing. Despite her initial worries, the visit was going well. Mrs. Bennet was predictably enthusiastic, but Darcy's patient manner soothed any lingering concerns. Mr. Bennet, meanwhile, contented himself with quiet observations, occasionally offering a wry comment that brought a smile to Elizabeth's face.

Later, as Elizabeth sat with her father in the library, she asked, "What do you think of Pemberley, Papa?"

Mr. Bennet leaned back in his chair, his eyes twinkling with amusement. "It is as grand as I expected, though I must say, my dear, it is not the house that impresses me most."

Elizabeth raised an eyebrow. "Oh? And what does, if not the grandeur of Pemberley?"

Mr. Bennet smiled softly. "It is you, Lizzy. You are growing into your role here with such grace. I admit I was concerned at first that such a place might overwhelm you, but I see now that you are more than capable of mastering it."

Elizabeth's heart swelled at her father's rare words of praise. "Thank you, Papa. That means more to me than you know."

He waved a hand dismissively, though she could see the affection in his eyes. "You've always been more than I deserved, Lizzy."

Later, as Elizabeth watched her parents retire to their rooms for the evening, she felt a profound sense of peace. Despite her initial nervousness, the visit was going smoothly, and she was glad to have her family at Pemberley. This grand estate, which had once seemed intimidating, now felt complete with the people she loved filling its halls.

<u>Building Confidence</u>

With Jane's visit and her heartfelt confessions and her parents now returned to Longbourn, Elizabeth found a renewed sense of purpose. She resolved to embrace her role with confidence and grace. Her interactions with the staff became even more thoughtful, her management of the estate more assured. She took Mrs. Reynolds' advice to heart, trusting her instincts and believing in her capabilities.

Elizabeth also began to engage more actively with the tenants of Pemberley. She visited their homes, listened to their concerns, and worked alongside Mr. Darcy to ensure their well-being. Her genuine interest in their lives and her efforts to improve their conditions endeared her to the tenants, who began to see her as a true steward of Pemberley.

Elizabeth's relationship with Mr. Darcy continued to deepen. Their mutual respect and love for each other created a strong foundation for their marriage. They supported each other in their respective roles, finding joy in shared responsibilities and moments of quiet companionship.

Mr. Darcy's unwavering faith in Elizabeth bolstered her confidence. He often praised her efforts and celebrated her successes, both big and small. Their partnership was a source of strength and comfort for Elizabeth, helping her navigate the challenges of her new life.

As Elizabeth became more comfortable in her role, society's perception of her began to shift. Her genuine kindness, intelligence, and competence gradually won over many of her initial detractors.

The gossip and judgment that had once surrounded her marriage to Mr. Darcy started to fade, replaced by admiration and respect.

Elizabeth's social gatherings at Pemberley became well-regarded events. Her warmth and hospitality created an inviting atmosphere that guests appreciated. She forged new friendships and strengthened existing ones, building a supportive social network.

Even Lady Catherine de Bourgh, though still disapproving, began to grudgingly acknowledge Elizabeth's capabilities. While she never fully embraced Elizabeth as the Mistress of Pemberley, she could not deny the positive changes Elizabeth had brought to the estate.

During a particularly tense visit, Lady Catherine remarked, "I see that Pemberley is well-maintained, Mrs. Darcy. You have not entirely failed in your duties."

Elizabeth accepted the backhanded compliment with grace. She understood that Lady Catherine's approval was unlikely, but she took solace in the fact that even her most ardent critic could see the improvements she had made.

As the months passed, Elizabeth continued to grow into her role. She worked closely with Mrs. Reynolds to ensure the smooth running of the household, fostered positive relationships with the staff, and remained attentive to the needs of the tenants. Her confidence grew, and she found a deep sense of fulfilment in her responsibilities.

With Jane's impending motherhood, Elizabeth also began to think about her own future. The prospect of having children of her own filled her with both excitement and a touch of apprehension. She knew that motherhood would bring its own set of challenges, but she felt ready to face them with the same determination she had shown in her role as Mistress of Pemberley.

<u>Challenges and Triumphs</u>

Despite her growing confidence, Elizabeth's journey was not without its obstacles. There were moments of doubt and instances where her decisions were met with resistance. Managing such a large estate required constant vigilance and adaptability.

One particularly challenging situation arose when a severe storm damaged several cottages on the estate. The tenants were distressed, and the repairs required immediate attention. Elizabeth and Mr. Darcy worked tirelessly to coordinate the restoration efforts, ensuring that the affected families had temporary accommodations and that the repairs were completed swiftly.

Elizabeth's hands on approach and genuine concern for the tenants earned her further respect and admiration. She proved that she was not only capable but also compassionate, a true guardian of Pemberley's legacy.

Throughout these challenges, Elizabeth's bond with the staff continued to strengthen. Mrs. Reynolds remained a steadfast ally, offering guidance and support whenever needed. Elizabeth also developed close relationships with other key members of the household, such as the butler, the cook, the head gardener, and the stable master.

These relationships were built on mutual respect and trust. Elizabeth valued their expertise and contributions, and in turn, they appreciated her dedication and fairness. Together, they formed a cohesive team that worked harmoniously to maintain the high standards of Pemberley.

Elizabeth's experiences as Mistress of Pemberley also led to significant personal growth. She became more confident in her abilities, more assured in her decisions, and more empathetic in her interactions with others. The challenges she faced and the successes she achieved shaped her into a more resilient and capable woman.

She also learned the importance of balance. While her responsibilities as Mistress were demanding, Elizabeth made time for herself and her relationship with Mr. Darcy. They enjoyed quiet walks in the gardens, lively discussions in the library, and moments of shared laughter and affection.

These moments of connection and relaxation were vital for maintaining their bond and their well-being.

As the first year of her marriage drew nearer, Elizabeth reflected on all that she had accomplished. She had navigated the complexities of her new role, earned the respect of the staff and tenants, and strengthened her relationship with Mr. Darcy. She had faced her fears and doubts head-on, emerging stronger and more confident.

The future, though uncertain, no longer seemed as daunting. Elizabeth felt ready to embrace whatever challenges and opportunities lay ahead. With her husband by her side and the support of those around her, she was determined to uphold the legacy of Pemberley and create a bright and prosperous future for all who called it home.

The Seasons of Pemberley

When, Spring arrived at Pemberley with a burst of colour and new life. The gardens, meticulously tended by the gardeners, bloomed in a riot of flowers. Elizabeth found joy in the simple pleasures of the season—morning walks among the blossoms, afternoons spent planning new garden layouts, and evenings enjoying the fresh spring air with Mr. Darcy.

The arrival of spring also brought renewed energy to the estate. The tenants began preparing their fields for planting, and Elizabeth took an active interest in their efforts. She organised a community gathering to discuss agricultural improvements and share best practices. Her involvement and enthusiasm inspired the tenants, fostering a sense of unity and shared purpose.

Summer

As summer settled over Pemberley, the estate thrived under the warm sun. The fields were lush with crops, and the gardens were a testament to the hard work of the gardeners. Elizabeth revealed in the vibrancy of the season, hosting outdoor gatherings and picnics on the expansive lawns.

The longer days also provided opportunities for Elizabeth to delve deeper into the management of the estate. She and Mr. Darcy worked together to implement new strategies for improving agricultural yields and enhancing the well-being of the tenants. Their collaborative efforts strengthened their partnership and brought tangible benefits to Pemberley

Autumn

Autumn brought a sense of fulfilment as the fruits of labor were harvested. The estate buzzed with activity as crops were gathered, and preparations were made for the colder months ahead. Elizabeth oversaw the harvest celebrations, ensuring that the tenants and staff felt appreciated for their hard work.

The changing colours of the landscape prompted reflection. Elizabeth took time to consider all that had been accomplished and to plan for the future. She and Mr. Darcy discussed long-term goals for the estate, including educational opportunities for the tenants' children and initiatives to promote sustainability.

Winter

Even when, Winter enveloped Pemberley in a blanket of snow, creating a serene and tranquil atmosphere. The shorter days and longer nights provided an opportunity for rest and rejuvenation. Elizabeth enjoyed the coziness of the season, spending evenings by the fire with Mr. Darcy, reading, and sharing stories.

The winter months also tested the resilience of the estate. Harsh weather conditions required careful management of resources and attention to the needs of the tenants. Elizabeth worked closely with Mrs. Reynolds and the staff to ensure that everyone was well cared for during the coldest.

New Birth

As September arrived and the golden hues of autumn began to sweep across Pemberley's vast landscape, Elizabeth found her thoughts constantly drifting to Jane. The letters between the two sisters had been frequent, with Jane sharing her excitement and nervousness about the imminent arrival of her child. Though Jane was always calm and serene in her letters, Elizabeth sensed an undercurrent of anxiety in her sister's words. The birth of a first child was always a momentous occasion, and Jane, ever the gentle soul, would surely be comforted by familiar faces during such a significant time.

One morning, as Elizabeth sat by the window of her morning room, the cool breeze carrying the scent of the changing season, she felt a pang of worry. Jane's due date was approaching, and despite her outward calm, Elizabeth knew her sister must be feeling nervous. She reached for her quill and parchment, deciding it was time to offer her support in a more direct way.

"My dearest Jane," she began, her pen gliding across the paper. _"As your time draws near, I find myself thinking of you more and more. I know Bingley will be by your side, but if you would like me there as well, I would come at once. There is no place I would rather be than by your side during such an important moment. Please let me know, and if it is your wish, I will make the journey to Netherfield Park Park immediately. With all my love, Lizzy."_

Elizabeth sealed the letter and sent it off with haste, her heart already hoping Jane would ask her to be there. It wasn't long before a reply arrived, the sight of Jane's neat handwriting bringing a sense of relief to Elizabeth's heart.

"My dearest Lizzy," Jane's letter read. _"I would love nothing more than to have you by my side for the birth of my child. I have spoken with Mama, and she, too, wishes to be here. Please come as soon as you can, for your presence will bring me great comfort. I cannot tell you how much it would mean to me. With all my love, Jane."_

Elizabeth wasted no time. She spoke to Darcy that evening, expressing her desire to be with Jane at Netherfield Park for the birth. He was, as ever, understanding and supportive.

"Of course, you must go," Darcy said, taking her hand as they sat by the fire. "Jane will need you, and I know how close the two of you are. You will be a great source of strength for her."

Elizabeth smiled at him, grateful for his unwavering support. "Thank you, Fitzwilliam. I only hope I can be of help to her."

With Darcy's encouragement, Elizabeth quickly made arrangements to leave for Netherfield Park. Mrs. Bennet, upon hearing of Jane's request for both of them to be present, had already packed her bags and was eagerly preparing for the journey. Elizabeth could imagine her mother's excited chatter as she prepared to welcome her first grandchild, and though the thought amused her, she was also grateful that Mrs. Bennet's presence would comfort Jane in its own way.

When Elizabeth and Mrs. Bennet arrived at Netherfield Park, the household was in a state of quiet anticipation. Jane's serene nature seemed to have settled over the place, and despite the tension that often accompanied such occasions, there was an air of calm. Mr. Bingley, ever the doting husband, greeted Elizabeth with warmth, his usual good-natured smile still present despite his obvious concern for Jane.

"Thank you for coming, Elizabeth," Bingley said as he led her into the house. "Jane has been eager for your arrival, and I must admit, having you and Mrs. Bennet here has brought her great comfort."

Elizabeth smiled, touched by his sincerity. "I wouldn't be anywhere else, Charles. How is she?"

Bingley's expression softened. "She is resting for now, but she has been in good spirits. I know she'll be relieved to see you."

Elizabeth made her way upstairs, where Jane was resting in her room. When she entered, she found her sister sitting by the window, looking as radiant as ever despite her obvious exhaustion. Jane's face lit up the moment she saw Elizabeth.

"Lizzy!" Jane exclaimed, reaching out her hand. "Oh, I'm so glad you're here."

Elizabeth hurried to her side, embracing her gently. "I wouldn't have missed this for the world, Jane. How are you feeling?"

Jane smiled, her calm manner belying the weight of the moment. "A little tired, but well. Bingley has been wonderful, and I'm so happy to have you and Mama here."

The days that followed were filled with quiet anticipation as the household waited for the baby's arrival. Mrs. Bennet, of course, was a flurry of excitement, often found hovering near Jane's room, chattering endlessly about what the child might look like and how grand it would be to have a little Bingley heir. Elizabeth, though amused by her mother's enthusiasm, kept her focus on supporting Jane, spending as much time with her sister as possible.

When the moment finally came, it was in the still hours of the night. Elizabeth woke to the sound of soft murmurs in the hall, and within minutes, the household was quietly bustling. Elizabeth, with Bingley's blessing, stayed by Jane's side throughout the labour, her hand clasped tightly in her sister's as she whispered words of comfort and encouragement.

The hours were long, but Jane was strong, her quiet determination shining through. Bingley hovered anxiously nearby, but the presence of Elizabeth and Mrs. Bennet seemed to ease his nerves. Elizabeth marvelled at her sister's calm strength, and though the process was difficult, Jane faced it with the grace that had always defined her.

Finally, just as the first light of dawn began to break through the curtains, the cries of a newborn filled the room. Jane, exhausted but radiant, smiled weakly as the midwife placed the baby in her arms.

"It's a girl," the midwife announced with a soft smile. "A healthy, beautiful girl."

Tears filled Elizabeth's eyes as she looked at the tiny, perfect child in her sister's arms. Jane gazed down at her daughter with a mixture of awe and overwhelming love, her exhaustion momentarily forgotten.

"Charlotte Jane," Jane whispered, her voice full of tenderness. "Her name is Charlotte Jane."

Elizabeth's heart swelled at the sound of the name, and she leaned down to kiss her sister's cheek. "She's perfect, Jane."

Bingley, who had been watching in quiet awe, stepped forward, his eyes shining with pride. He gently took his wife's hand and gazed at their daughter with a look of pure joy. "She is perfect," he agreed softly.

The room was filled with a sense of peace and joy as the new family welcomed their daughter into the world. Elizabeth stood back, watching the scene unfold with a heart full of gratitude and happiness for her beloved sister. Charlotte Jane Bingley, with her delicate features and soft cries, was already surrounded by so much love.

—-

The days following Charlotte's birth were filled with happiness. Jane recovered well, and Bingley was a doting father from the very start. Mrs. Bennet, of course, could scarcely contain her pride, spending much of her time cooing over her new granddaughter and boasting to anyone who would listen about the birth of little Charlotte Jane.

Elizabeth stayed on at Netherfield Park for a time, helping Jane with the baby and enjoying the new sense of family that had blossomed with the arrival of her niece. Every time she held Charlotte in her arms, Elizabeth felt an overwhelming sense of love for the child and pride for her sister. The bond between the sisters, always strong, had deepened even further.

As the leaves of autumn continued to fall outside the windows of Netherfield Park, Elizabeth found herself thinking often of Darcy and Pemberley, but she knew she was exactly where she needed to be. Soon enough, she would return to her own life as Mistress of Pemberley, but for now, her place was here—by Jane's side, welcoming the newest member of their family into the world.

Returning Home

Elizabeth returned to Pemberley with a heart full of joy and memories from her time at Netherfield Park. The carriage ride home had been peaceful, giving her time to reflect on the love she had witnessed between Jane, Bingley, and their newborn daughter, Charlotte Jane. The days spent with her sister had been a blessing, and now, as Pemberley's grand silhouette appeared on the horizon, Elizabeth felt a wave of contentment wash over her.

The sun was beginning to set when she arrived, casting a golden glow over the estate, and Darcy was waiting for her at the entrance, as he always did when she had been away. His tall figure stood against the backdrop of the grand house, his expression one of quiet anticipation. As the carriage stopped, Elizabeth felt her heart quicken, as it often did when she saw him after time apart. Darcy stepped forward, offering his hand to help her down, and the warmth in his gaze spoke of how much he had missed her.

"Welcome home, my love," he said softly, his voice filled with affection as she stepped into his embrace.

Elizabeth smiled up at him, her eyes shining with happiness. "Oh, Fitzwilliam, it's so good to be home. But I must tell you—Jane and Charles are overjoyed, and I am an aunt to the most beautiful baby girl. They have named her Charlotte Jane."

Darcy's smile broadened at the news, his expression softening as he saw the joy radiating from his wife. "Charlotte Jane," he repeated thoughtfully. "A lovely name, for what I am sure is a lovely child."

Elizabeth nodded, her face alight with emotion. "She is perfect, Fitzwilliam. Jane and Charles are so happy, and little Charlotte is already the light of their lives." She paused for a moment, her voice lowering with affection. "It was such a privilege to be there, to witness it all."

Darcy gently brushed a stray lock of hair from her face, his touch tender. He could see the love and longing in her eyes—the deep bond she shared with her sister, and now with her niece. Though

Elizabeth had returned to Pemberley, part of her heart remained at Netherfield Park, in the soft glow of family.

"You have always spoken of the love between your sister and Bingley," Darcy said, his voice thoughtful. "I can only imagine how much more complete their happiness must feel now." He paused, his gaze searching hers as a soft smile touched his lips. "One day, my love. One day, we shall know that same joy."

Elizabeth felt a warmth spread through her chest at his words, her heart swelling with emotion. She reached up to cup his face, her eyes filled with gratitude for the man who had not only given her his heart but also understood her deepest hopes without her ever having to say them aloud.

"Yes," she whispered, her voice steady with the certainty that only Darcy could inspire in her. "One day."

Together, they walked inside, where the flickering candlelight cast a soft glow over the familiar halls of Pemberley. The quiet grandeur of the estate welcomed Elizabeth back into its embrace, and as she and Darcy settled into their evening routine, the weight of all she had witnessed at Netherfield Park stayed with her, like a gentle hum of anticipation.

Over the following days, Elizabeth shared every detail of her time with Jane and Bingley. At dinner, she would tell Darcy about the peaceful atmosphere of Netherfield Park, how Jane had taken to motherhood with such grace, and how Bingley had been a doting and proud father from the moment Charlotte was born.

"It was a sight to behold," Elizabeth remarked one evening, a smile playing on her lips as she recalled Bingley's unabashed joy. "He could scarcely stop gazing at Charlotte. Every time she made the slightest movement, he was there, ready to tend to her as if she were the most fragile thing in the world."

Darcy chuckled, his expression one of amusement mixed with warmth. "I can imagine Bingley in such a state. His heart is as open and good-natured as any man's can be. Charlotte is fortunate to have such parents."

Elizabeth nodded, resting her chin on her hand as she looked at her husband. "Yes, she is. And I couldn't help but think of us—how it will be when our time comes."

Darcy's eyes softened at her words. He reached across the table, taking her hand in his. "It will be a joy beyond measure," he said simply. "And you, Elizabeth, will be the most wonderful mother."

Elizabeth's heart fluttered at his words, the depth of his love and his faith in her always managing to stir something deep within her. "And you, Fitzwilliam, will be the kindest of fathers," she replied, her voice full of conviction. "I have no doubt of it."

They sat in companionable silence for a moment, the flickering candlelight casting soft shadows over their faces. The future seemed brighter than ever, filled with promise and love. Pemberley, with its grandeur and beauty, had always felt like a place of endless possibility, and now Elizabeth saw it not just as a great estate, but as the home where their family would grow.

The First Anniversary

As Elizabeth and Mr. Darcy celebrated their first wedding anniversary, they reflected on the journey they had undertaken together. The challenges they had faced and the triumphs they had achieved had strengthened their bond and deepened their love. Their celebration was a quiet and intimate affair, filled with gratitude and hope for the future.

The arrival of Jane's first child in September, brought immense joy to both the Bingley and Darcy families. Elizabeth traveled to Netherfield Park to be by her sister's side, offering support and sharing in the happiness of the new arrival. Holding her newborn niece in her arms, Elizabeth felt a profound sense of love and connection.

Jane's experience as a new mother also inspired Elizabeth to think about her own future. She and Mr. Darcy discussed their hopes for a family, sharing dreams of the life they wanted to create for their children. The prospect of motherhood, once a source of apprehension, now filled Elizabeth with anticipation and excitement.

Looking ahead, Elizabeth felt ready to embrace whatever the future held. She had proven to herself and to others that she was a capable and compassionate steward of Pemberley's legacy. With the support of her husband, her family, and the community she had come to cherish, Elizabeth was poised to create a bright and prosperous future for Pemberley and all who called it home.

Elizabeth Darcy, had truly become the Mistress of Pemberley, in every sense of the title. She had faced the expectations, worries, and judgments head-on, emerging stronger and more assured. Her journey was a testament to her character and her love for her husband and their shared home. Pemberley, under her stewardship, was not just a grand estate but a living, breathing community where kindness, respect, and love flourished.

As the months passed, life at Pemberley settled into a peaceful rhythm. Elizabeth wrote regularly to Jane, always eager to hear about Charlotte's progress and Jane's experiences as a mother. In return, Jane's letters were filled with anecdotes about their little girl—her first smiles, the way she would quiet whenever Bingley held her, and the happiness that filled their home.

Darcy, too, found himself often thinking of his own future as a father. Though he had never voiced it openly, the sight of Elizabeth's joy when she spoke of Charlotte stirred something within him. The thought of raising children with her, of filling Pemberley's halls with the laughter of their own little ones, became more vivid with each passing day.

One afternoon, as Elizabeth walked through the gardens of Pemberley with Darcy by her side, the late autumn air crisp around them, she turned to him with a smile.

"Do you remember when we first walked here, Fitzwilliam?" she asked, her voice soft with the weight of memory. "When I saw Pemberley for the first time?"

Darcy smiled, his eyes warm as he looked at her. "How could I forget? It was the day everything changed for me."

Elizabeth's heart swelled with love for him. "I never imagined, when I first stepped foot here, that this would become my home—our home. And now, I cannot picture my life anywhere else."

Darcy stopped walking and turned to face her fully, taking both her hands in his. "Pemberley has always been grand, Elizabeth, but you are the one who has made it feel like home." He paused, his gaze searching hers. "And one day, it will be even more complete—with children to fill these halls with laughter."

Elizabeth smiled, the warmth of his words enveloping her like a gentle embrace. "Yes," she whispered. "One day."

And in that moment, with the golden autumn light casting its glow around them, the future felt as bright and full of promise as it ever had.

Jane's Second Visit

Several months after Jane's first visit, she returned to Pemberley with her infant daughter. Elizabeth welcomed her sister and niece with open arms, thrilled to have Jane's company once more. Jane's arrival brought a renewed sense of family and comfort to Pemberley.

The sisters spent their days reminiscing about their childhood, sharing stories of their husbands, and marvelling at the changes in their lives. Elizabeth delighted in playing with her niece, Charlotte Jane, finding joy in the simple pleasures of watching the child grow and develop, in the May sunshine.

One evening, after the baby had been put to bed, Jane and Elizabeth sat by the fire in Elizabeth's private sitting room. The warmth of the fire and the soft glow of the candles created an intimate atmosphere, perfect for heartfelt conversation.

"Lizzy," Jane began, "you have done wonderfully here at Pemberley. I can see the respect the staff and tenants have for you. You have truly made this place your home."

Elizabeth smiled, her heart swelling with pride and gratitude. "Thank you, Jane. Your support has meant the world to me. I often think of our conversations and the advice you have given me."

Jane reached out and took Elizabeth's hand. "We have always been there for each other, and we always will be. I want you to know that you can confide in me about anything. We are sisters, and nothing will ever change that."

Elizabeth squeezed Jane's hand, feeling a profound sense of connection. "There is something I have been meaning to tell you, Jane. I am with child,"

Jane's eyes widened with joy. "Oh, Lizzy! That is the most wonderful news! I am so happy for you and Mr. Darcy."

Elizabeth's smile was radiant. "Thank you, Jane. I am excited but also a little nervous. There is so much to consider and prepare for. I want to be the best

mother I can be. I am due at around Christmas, when you are all here."

Jane nodded, understanding Elizabeth's feelings all too well. "You will be a wonderful mother, Lizzy. You have a kind heart and a strong spirit. And you have Mr. Darcy by your side. Together, you will create a loving and nurturing home for your child."

The sisters embraced, their bond stronger than ever. Elizabeth felt a renewed sense of hope and anticipation for the future. She was ready to embrace the joys and challenges of motherhood, knowing that she had the love and support of her family.

New Responsibilities

As Elizabeth's pregnancy progressed, she took on new responsibilities with enthusiasm and care. She and Mr. Darcy prepared for the arrival of their child, making sure that every detail was attended to. The nursery was decorated with love and thoughtfulness, filled with soft fabrics and beautiful furnishings.

Elizabeth also sought advice from Jane and Mrs. Reynolds, who both provided valuable insights and guidance. Jane shared her experiences as a new mother, offering practical tips and emotional support. Mrs. Reynolds, with her years of wisdom, helped Elizabeth navigate the preparations with confidence.

During this time, Elizabeth's bond with the staff at Pemberley deepened. They rallied around her, offering their support and well-wishes. The maids took extra care in preparing the nursery, the cook made sure Elizabeth had nutritious meals, and the gardeners brought fresh flowers to brighten her days.

Elizabeth's genuine appreciation for their efforts further endeared her to the staff. She made it a point to express her gratitude and acknowledge their contributions. This mutual respect and affection created a harmonious and supportive environment within the household.

As news of Elizabeth's pregnancy spread, society's reception was overwhelmingly positive. The initial skepticism and judgment that had once surrounded her marriage to Mr. Darcy had faded, replaced by admiration and respect. Elizabeth's kindness, competence, and dedication had won over many hearts.

Social engagements at Pemberley were now well attended and highly regarded. Elizabeth's warmth and hospitality created an inviting atmosphere, and guests enjoyed the lively and engaging events she hosted. Her growing family only added to the joy and excitement surrounding Pemberley.

As Elizabeth entered the final months of her pregnancy, she faced new challenges. Her health became a concern, and she experienced periods of fatigue and discomfort. Mr. Darcy, ever attentive and caring, ensured that she had the best medical care and encouraged her to rest and take care of herself.

Despite these challenges, Elizabeth remained positive and focused. She relied on the support of her family and the staff at Pemberley, who were always ready to assist her. Her determination and resilience were evident, and she approached each day with grace and courage.

Lady Catherine's Return

In the midst of these challenges, Lady Catherine de Bourgh made another visit to Pemberley. Her disapproval of Elizabeth had not waned, and she made no effort to hide her critical nature. Lady Catherine questioned Elizabeth's ability to handle the responsibilities of motherhood and manage the estate.

"Mrs. Darcy," Lady Catherine said with a condescending tone, "I trust you are aware of the demands that will come with a child. Pemberley requires constant attention, and I wonder if you can manage both."

Elizabeth, though hurt by the remarks, remained composed. "Lady Catherine, I am fully aware of the responsibilities I bear, both as Mistress of Pemberley and as a mother. I am confident that with the support of my husband and the capable staff, I can meet these challenges."

Lady Catherine's expression remained stern, but she could not refute Elizabeth's determination. The visit, though tense, did not shake Elizabeth's resolve. She knew that proving herself to Lady Catherine was a difficult, if not impossible, task. Instead, she focused on the positive support she received from her loved ones, but was pleased when Lady Catherine returned to Rosings Park.

A Baby is Born

The week before Christmas, on the seventeenth of December, finally Elizabeth gave birth to a healthy baby boy. William, The joy and relief that filled Pemberley were immeasurable. Mr. Darcy was overjoyed, and the entire household celebrated the new addition to the family.

Elizabeth's strength and resilience during the labour were admired by all. She and Mr. Darcy named their son William, after Mr. Darcy's father. The baby's arrival marked a new beginning for the Darcy family, bringing a sense of completeness and fulfilment.

As Elizabeth settled into her role as a mother, she found a new sense of purpose and joy. The challenges of caring for a newborn were balanced by the overwhelming love she felt for her son. Elizabeth embraced the sleepless nights, the constant feedings, and the endless diaper changes with a smile.

Her relationship with Mr. Darcy deepened further as they navigated parenthood together. They shared the responsibilities, supported each other through the challenges, and cherished the moments of joy and wonder that their son brought into their lives.

With the addition of their son, Elizabeth and Mr. Darcy felt a renewed sense of responsibility to uphold the legacy of Pemberley. They were determined to create a nurturing and loving environment for their child, ensuring that Pemberley remained a place of warmth and hospitality.

Elizabeth continued to manage the estate with the same dedication and care she had always shown. She balanced her responsibilities as Mistress of Pemberley with her new role as a mother, finding harmony in her dual roles.

As Elizabeth looked ahead to the future, she felt a profound sense of fulfilment and optimism. She had faced and overcome numerous challenges, grown into her role as Mistress of Pemberley, and embraced the joys of motherhood. Her journey had been one of growth, resilience, and transformation.

With her husband by her side, her beloved sister Jane's support, and the strength of the Pemberley community, Elizabeth was ready to face whatever the future held. The legacy of Pemberley was secure, and the Darcy family's future was bright.

The Darcy family continued to thrive, with Elizabeth and Mr. Darcy's love serving as the foundation of their happiness. Their son William grew up surrounded by the beauty and legacy of Pemberley, instilled with the values of kindness, respect, and responsibility.

Elizabeth's bond with Jane and her family remained strong, and their children grew up as close cousins and friends. The families shared many joyous occasions, celebrating milestones and supporting each other through life's challenges.

Elizabeth's commitment to Pemberley extended beyond the manor house. She continued to build strong relationships with the tenants and workers on the estate. Elizabeth organised regular gatherings where the tenants could voice their concerns and share their ideas for improving the community.

One such gathering led to the establishment of a small school for the children of the estate. Elizabeth worked tirelessly to ensure that the school was well- equipped and staffed with capable teachers.

The education of the children became a passion project for her, reflecting her belief in the importance of knowledge and opportunity.

The staff at Pemberley had become an extended family to Elizabeth. She valued their hard work and dedication and made it a point to show her appreciation. Elizabeth introduced a system of rewards and recognitions, celebrating milestones and achievements within the household.

Elizabeth's attentiveness fostered a strong sense of loyalty among the staff. They felt respected and valued, and this positive atmosphere translated into their work. Pemberley ran smoothly and efficiently, a testament to the harmonious relationships within the household.

As the years passed, Pemberley thrived, its halls once again filled with the warmth of family, laughter, and the deep-rooted love between Elizabeth and Darcy. The estate, which had long stood as a symbol of wealth and grandeur, now became a true home—a place of comfort and joy for all who resided there. Elizabeth, having secured her place as Mistress of Pemberley, found herself deeply content in the life she had built with Darcy.

The arrival of their son, William, had been a moment of profound happiness for both Elizabeth and Darcy. The birth of a male heir ensured the continuation of the Darcy line, but more than that, it filled their hearts with a love neither had ever known before. From the moment they first held baby William in their arms, they knew their family was complete. The little boy had inherited his father's strong features and calm disposition, but there was a glint of Elizabeth's lively spirit in his eyes, something that delighted both his parents.

Elizabeth embraced motherhood with the same strength and grace she had always shown, guiding her son with love and care. She would spend her mornings walking through Pemberley's gardens with William in her arms, pointing out the flowers and birds, introducing him to the beauty of the world. Darcy, ever the doting father, would often join them, his presence a constant source of support and comfort. The quiet moments they shared as a family in the gardens, or by the grand hearth in the drawing room, became Elizabeth's most cherished memories.

Pemberley, too, reflected the happiness of its inhabitants. Under Elizabeth's care, with the help of Mrs. Reynolds and the staff, the estate had blossomed into a place of beauty and warmth. Its once austere atmosphere had softened, and Elizabeth's touch could be seen in every corner, from the bright, welcoming rooms to the well-tended gardens. The tenants, too, benefited from the kindness of their new Mistress, as Elizabeth took an active interest in their well-being, making sure that Pemberley was not just an estate but a thriving community.

As for Lady Catherine de Bourgh, though her initial disapproval of Elizabeth had been fierce, time had tempered her sharp tongue. Lady Catherine had been furious when Darcy had married beneath his station, as she had often reminded him, but even she could not deny the undeniable happiness that had bloomed between Darcy and Elizabeth. After the birth of young William, Lady Catherine's visits became less frequent, and when she did call upon Pemberley, her manner was cooler but more restrained.

Elizabeth, however, never let her guard down around Lady Catherine. She had learned to navigate the older woman's barbed comments with grace and patience, always remembering that while Lady Catherine's opinions were strong, they no longer held any real power over her. Darcy, for his part, remained steadfast in his support of Elizabeth, ensuring that Lady Catherine knew her influence over him had waned.

There were, of course, the occasional sharp glances and subtle remarks from Lady Catherine about Pemberley's management or the raising of young William. But Elizabeth, with her wit and her ever-growing confidence in her role as mistress, knew how to handle these moments with the skill of a seasoned diplomat. She could smile through Lady Catherine's cutting remarks and answer with such poise that the dowager, for all her attempts at superiority, found herself often at a loss for words.

Despite Lady Catherine's reframed attitude, there was always an undercurrent of tension in their interactions. Elizabeth knew that Lady Catherine would never fully accept her as Darcy's equal, but she no longer needed her approval. She had found strength in her position at Pemberley, in the love she shared with Darcy, and in the joy she took from raising their son. Lady Catherine's opinions, once a source of anxiety, had become nothing more than distant echoes, unable to disturb the harmony of Elizabeth's life.

The Darcy Family

As the years went by, Pemberley continued to flourish under the careful stewardship of Elizabeth and Darcy. Their family grew closer, with young William becoming the pride of his parents. He was a lively child, full of curiosity and warmth, and he often brought laughter to the once-serene halls of Pemberley. Elizabeth watched with pride as Darcy taught their son the ways of the estate, passing on the knowledge that would one day make William a worthy heir.

The estate itself, restored to its full glory, became a symbol not just of wealth and power, but of love and family. The once-empty rooms were now filled with life, and the staff, who had grown fond of Elizabeth, took great pride in serving a household so full of joy. Visitors to Pemberley remarked not just on its grandeur, but on the warmth that seemed to radiate from within its walls, a testament to the love that had blossomed between Elizabeth and Darcy.

Elizabeth's family, too, often visited Pemberley. Jane and Bingley, with their growing brood of children, were frequent guests, and Elizabeth cherished the time spent with her sister. The sight of their children playing together in the gardens of Pemberley brought a sense of fulfilment to Elizabeth's heart. She and Jane, who had once dreamed of love and happiness in their youth, now had it in abundance, and their bond remained as strong as ever.

Even Mrs. Bennet, though still prone to the occasional outburst of excitement, had mellowed somewhat, content with the knowledge that both of her daughters had married well and secured their futures. Mr. Bennet, ever the quiet observer, took great pleasure in visiting Pemberley, often retreating to Darcy's library, where the two men would spend hours in comfortable silence, each with a book in hand.

As the years rolled on, Elizabeth would often find herself standing at the windows of Pemberley, watching the changing seasons with a sense of quiet gratitude. The life she had built here, with the man she loved and the family they had created, was more than she could have ever dreamed.

She thought back to the first time she had visited Pemberley, when she had seen the house and grounds with fresh eyes, not knowing then that it would one day become her home. The journey that had brought her here—from the lively days at Longbourn, to the misunderstandings and revelations with Darcy, to the fulfilment she now felt as Mistress of Pemberley—had been filled with challenges and joys alike.

Now, standing at the heart of the home she had made her own, with baby William resting peacefully in his crib, Elizabeth knew she had everything she had ever wanted. Pemberley was not just an estate, nor was it just a symbol of wealth or prestige. It was a place of love, a place where family could grow and flourish. It was the home she and Darcy had built together, the legacy they would one day pass on to their children.

Elizabeth turned from the window, her gaze resting on Darcy, who stood nearby, watching her with that same quiet affection she had come to cherish. He walked over to her, taking her hand in his, and together they stood in the soft glow of the firelight, their hearts full, their future bright.

Pemberley was restored, not just in its physical beauty, but in its soul. And Elizabeth, who had once stepped into this grand house with both fear and excitement, now knew it was where she truly belonged.

With a beautiful home, a loving husband, and a family of her own, Elizabeth Darcy had found her place in the world.

The story of Pemberley was one of love, endurance, and the quiet triumph of a woman who had found her strength not in titles or wealth, but in the heart of her family. And in that, Elizabeth knew, she had found her true happiness.

The End

<u>About the Author</u>

Darryl Martel - Delve into a realm where imagination knows no bounds, where the ethereal dance of words paints vivid tapestries of the mind. Through the nimble strokes of storytelling, I navigate realms both real and fantastical, crafting narratives that whisper secrets of the human condition. Each word is a brushstroke, each sentence a melody, weaving together a tapestry of emotion, intrigue, and revelation.